Also by Cynthia Rylant

Appalachia: The Voices of Sleeping Birds

God Got a Dog

Gooseberry Park

Gooseberry Park and the Master Plan

The Henry & Mudge series

Life

Missing May

The Mr. Putter & Tabby series

The Old Woman Who Named Things

The Van Gogh Cafe

When I Was Young in the Mountains

Rosetown

Cynthia Rylant

BEACH LANE BOOKS
New York London Toronto Sydney New Delhi

BEACH LANE BOOKS

An imprint of Simon & Schuster Children's Publishing Division

1230 Avenue of the Americas, New York, New York 10020

This book is a work of fiction. Any references to historical events, real people, or real places are used fictitiously. Other names, characters, places, and events are products of the author's imagination, and any resemblance to actual events or places or persons, living or dead, is entirely coincidental.

Text copyright © 2018 by Cynthia Rylant

Cover illustrations copyright © 2018 by Lori Richmond

All rights reserved, including the right of reproduction in whole or in part in any form.

BEACH LANE BOOKS is a trademark of Simon & Schuster, Inc.

For information about special discounts for bulk purchases, please contact Simon & Schuster Special Sales at 1-866-506-1949 or business@simonandschuster.com.

The Simon & Schuster Speakers Bureau can bring authors to your live event. For more information or to book an event, contact the Simon & Schuster Speakers Bureau at 1-866-248-3049 or visit our website at www.simonspeakers.com.

Also available in a Beach Lane Books hardcover edition

Book design by Irene Metaxatos

The text for this book was set in ITC Century Std.

Manufactured in the United States of America

0419 OPM

First Beach Lane Books paperback edition May 2019

10 9 8 7 6 5 4 3 2

The Library of Congress has cataloged the hardcover edition as follows:

Library of Congress Cataloging-in-Publication Data

Names: Rylant, Cynthia, author.

Title: Rosetown / Cynthia Rylant.

Description: First edition. | New York : Beach Lane Books, [2018] | Summary: In 1972, Flora Smallwood, nine, copes with her parents' separation with the help of her friends, Yury and Nessie, a new pet, and the familiar routines of life in Rosetown, Indiana.

Identifiers: LCCN 2017023378 | ISBN 9781534412774 (hardcover : alk. paper) | ISBN 9781534412781 (pbk) | ISBN 9781534412798 (e-book)

Subjects: | CYAC: Friendship—Fiction. | Family life—Indiana—Fiction. | City and town life—Fiction. | Books and reading—Fiction. | Indiana—History—20th century—Fiction. | BISAC: JUVENILE FICTION / Girls & Women. | JUVENILE FICTION / Social Issues / Friendship.

Classification: LCC PZ7.R982 Ros 2018 | DDC [Fic]—dc23 LC record available at https://lccn.loc.gov/2017023378

1

Wings and a Chair Used Books was where Flora Smallwood's mother worked three afternoons a week. Inside, it had a purple velveteen chair by the window for anyone who wanted to stay awhile, and Flora, who sometimes felt quite acutely the stress of being nine years old, and sensitive, loved this chair. Mondays, Wednesdays, and Fridays were her favorite days because of it.

The owner of the shop was Miss Meriwether, a tall woman with deep black hair pulled tightly into a ponytail. Miss Meriwether told Flora that in her younger days she had been a free spirit but that one day she'd decided to grow up and open a shop.

Flora tried to imagine Miss Meriwether as a free spirit, but it wasn't easy, as the words "inventory" and "bottom line" sometimes floated through the bookshop air as Flora sat reading. But Miss Meriwether did like long flowery skirts, so maybe she was still free in her heart.

Flora's family had been through a time of sadness, for their old, loving dog, Laurence, had passed away one spring night while everyone was sleeping. They all knew Laurence was fading. But no one believed, really, that he would ever not be with them anymore. Especially Flora, who had held on to his collar ever since she took her first steps.

But he did: he left them. And since then the idea of a new family pet sometimes had been mentioned. Yet never followed through on. Everyone was, in some way, still holding on to Laurence's collar.

Flora was an only child, and her parents were, for now, living in separate homes. The challenges of this, of course, were many. And there was the practical challenge for Flora of having two homes, with her own bedroom in each, for since most things do not come in duplicate, often the one thing she needed right that minute was not in this home, it was in the other. Sometimes the thing was not that important, as in the case of her green scarf or striped coat. But sometimes even something small like that—a scarf or a coat—suddenly felt so vital to her, and she felt a great sad longing because it was not in this home but the other one.

Flora's father, Forster Smallwood, worked for the Rosetown newspaper, *The Rosetown Chronicle*, and he was, Flora thought, a nice man, a good father, and a lost soul. She was not sure why she thought he was lost. Maybe it was the look she often saw on his face, that look that detached him from wherever he was and whatever he was doing and put him somewhere else. Maybe Neptune.

But he was a good father and a good photographer, too. He often allowed Flora to stand with him in his darkroom to watch a photograph slowly come into being. Standing under the red glow of the darkroom light, Flora watched the blank photographic paper bathe in the pan of chemicals. And then the formerly invisible face of a person would begin to materialize on the wet paper, his features becoming clear and strong, like a ghost who has suddenly found teeth and eyes and ears and put them on.

Both Flora's father and mother had been very troubled by the war in Vietnam, and now American soldiers were being withdrawn from the fighting. Rosetown, Indiana, in 1972 was like any other small American town, its citizens sharply divided over the war and what it all had been about. Flora's father once told her, when he was in a dark mood after the evening television news, "You were born into an angry world."

But then he had smiled, as if he realized how harsh this might have sounded, and he added, "Thank goodness you showed up just when we needed you."

It seemed to Flora that the purple velveteen chair by the window in Wings and a Chair Used Books was more important than ever these days. Laurence had passed on. Her scarves and coats were confused.

And fourth grade at Rosetown Primary School was so very different from third.

2

What Flora noticed at once on the first day of fourth grade had been the sudden confidence all of the former third graders seemed to have found, and she wondered where they had found it. Nearly all of her classmates appeared to be taller, louder, stronger, and possessed of a sureness of opinion that had been entirely absent the year before. The stumblers, the wanderers, and the floaters of third grade had suddenly, mysteriously, found their feet. They weren't afraid of school anymore. Or maybe of anything.

All of this made Flora a little shy. She missed the uncertainty.

Fortunately, a new and uncertain person had arrived in room 22, and with him Flora was beginning to build that precious thing called friendship.

His name was Yury, which set him apart right away. His Eastern European name, combined with the burden of being the new boy, made Yury a very uncertain fourth-grade person indeed.

He wore large round glasses, which made him look rather owl-like.

And he was very smart, like an owl, beneath all of the new-boy uncertainty. Flora knew this right away because he was clever. Clever the way her father was clever. Yury could look at a situation and in one or two sentences say all that needed saying about it. But he shared his cleverness with only one person in fourth grade: Flora. He sat behind her in class, so it was easy for him to whisper to the back of her head. Yury whispered, Flora smiled, and the seeds of friendship were planted.

They walked the same route after school three

afternoons a week. Yury walked to his father's office on State Street, and Flora walked to the bookshop on Main.

Yury's father was a doctor.

"Do you help in the office?" Flora asked one day as they walked their route together.

"My father has given me the job of making tea for everyone," Yury answered.

"Even for the patients?" asked Flora.

"Yes," said Yury. "It is healthy tea which is called Mo's 24."

"That doesn't sound very healthy," said Flora. "It should be called Tea for Long Life."

"The 24 are twenty-four herbs," explained Yury.

"Well, then, who is Mo?" asked Flora.

"Oh, he's Curly's brother," said Yury, grinning.

"He is not." Flora laughed. "I didn't know that the Three Stooges were popular in the Ukraine," she said.

"Even Ukrainians need their yuks," said Yury.

How strange, thought Flora, to be walking in

Rosetown with a Ukrainian boy who served tea in a doctor's office every afternoon, the doctor being his father.

She had told Yury about Laurence's passing. Yury had also said good-bye to an old pet, a cat whose name was Juliette, so he understood. Flora enjoyed Yury's company, but she especially appreciated his compassion.

When they reached the bookshop, Flora and Yury stood together in front of the window and inspected the week's display.

"I would like to go there," Yury said, pointing to a book about Key West. "I would sail a sailboat."

"And follow an octopus," said Flora.

"To South America," said Yury.

"To find a town filled with . . . ," Flora said, then waited for his answer.

"Elephants," finished Yury.

"You could write a book about them, and Miss Meriwether could put it in this window," said Flora.

"And we could stand here on the sidewalk together and look at it," Yury said.

Flora smiled.

She was starting to feel more certain, knowing Yury.

3

The days of a newspaper photographer in a small Indiana town were not often very exciting ones. But Flora's father once told her that every now and then there was "something of the cosmic experience." And on those occasions he liked to bring her along.

But it also had to be a Saturday.

Life did not often combine cosmic experiences with Saturdays in Rosetown, but on this particular Saturday it did. It was Flora's weekend at the yellow house, so Flora's father had to drive by and collect her.

After he called, she waited by the mailbox for him. When he pulled up, Flora got into the front seat and said, "What's up, bud?"

This was what she always said when her father invited her to come along on a job. It was a line from an old black-and-white movie they had once watched on television, about a newspaperman.

"Wait and see," her father said, which was what he always said.

They drove past the city limits, across the wide flat landscape of tall grasses shimmering yellow under the September sun, until, in the distance, Flora could see flashing red lights.

"It isn't scary, is it?" she asked softly. The red lights could mean something hard and awful.

"Oh no, dear," said her father. "I would never take you to scary."

Flora let go a deep breath. Good.

They pulled up behind a row of vehicles that included a police car, a TV news van, and a farmer on a tractor.

Flora's father smiled when he saw the tractor.

"Of course there would be a farmer," he said. "I love Indiana."

They parked and left their car, and soon the cosmic experience was right there in front of them.

Sitting on the ground was a parachutist who had experienced a hard landing, injuring a foot. But he was not the cosmic experience.

The cosmic experience was his parachuting companion, a little brown terrier wearing a red flight suit that was embroidered with one word: *Zowie.*

"That's Zowie," said Flora's father.

Flora was thrilled. She had not expected to meet a little dog who jumped out of airplanes, attached to his owner.

Zowie was sitting beside his adventurous owner as the policeman checked the condition of the young man's foot.

Zowie licked the policeman's hand.

"Zowie knows that's a good guy," said Flora.

Her father nodded.

"Wait here," he said. "I'll take some photos, and

then I'll ask if you can meet them."

Flora's father did his work while she waited quietly, apart from the action. Then he leaned over and said something to the parachutist. The young man nodded, grinned, and then waved Flora over to where he and Zowie sat.

Flora shyly went up to them. She said hello and asked if she could pet Zowie. The little dog danced around her feet.

"Brave dog," Flora said, smiling and petting his head.

"The best friend I've ever had," said the parachutist.

Oh yes, thought Flora. Yes. She understood.

On the drive back to Rosetown, Flora watched the dove-gray clouds move over the fields and farms. She looked toward the horizon dividing the brown soil from the blue sky. And deep inside she suddenly became aware of a feeling: *expectation.*

Something new was coming. Or maybe someone new.

She looked over at her father. Did he feel it

too? But his eyes, she could tell, were work eyes. Already he was developing the photographs in his mind.

The feeling was Flora's alone. She wondered about it all the way home.

4

Indiana was a beautiful place for a girl to grow. Flora always knew this. Her mother called it "balance."

"There is balance here in Indiana," Emma Jean Smallwood once said as they walked to the Windy Day Diner.

Naturally, this was a very vague statement, but Flora thought she understood its meaning. It had something to do with the harmony between earth and sky, with the way four country roads would converge at a crossroads, with the symmetry of a

white church in the center of town and the town
streets making perfect right angles to it.

Balance.

Flora's parents' separating had put her decidedly
off balance, yet the simple harmonies in the world
around her helped keep her feeling safe.

And she knew that her parents both loved her.
And that each of them loved the other. Flora had
never heard them fight. The feeling between them
was not one of war. It was instead as if they had
skipped the war completely and gone straight to
defeat, raising mutual flags of surrender. Then
came the dividing up of dishes, silverware, linens, and lamps so that one of them could live five
streets over.

Flora's father had brought old things for himself,
but he had bought new things for her room in the
white house. He said he wanted them to be "as good
as old," hoping she would feel as comfortable there
as in the yellow house.

She never quite was. But they had their old movies
on television to watch. And their popcorn popper.

Her parents had not told her how long this separation might last.

"We find we are a bit of a mess," her mother said. "And that we need to take some air."

Splitting one family into two was "taking air."

This had happened three months after Laurence passed, and Flora couldn't help wondering, if he had lived, would her parents not have needed air.

But she didn't want to hold Laurence responsible. He was seventeen when he decided not to wake up, which in dog years is ancient. He'd given them everything he had.

And Flora was still in the same town and in the same school, and she still had the same friends.

Like her friend Nessy.

Nessy and Flora had known each other for years. And though their families were very different, the two girls were very much alike.

They'd met in a summer reading club for children, ages four and five, at the Rosetown Free Library. Flora was five and Nessy was four, and each was a little worried about all of it, this reading club. On the day of the club's first meeting in the Children's Room, Nessy would not let go of her mother's hand when her mother wanted to go on some errands while the club had its meeting.

"It will be all right, Vanessa," said her mother, smiling while she tried to pry herself loose.

Another mother (who happened to be Emma Jean Smallwood) was standing nearby with her daughter, Flora. And Emma Jean said to Nessy, "'Vanessa' is the most beautiful name. I believe it means 'butterfly.' My daughter's name is Flora. It means 'flower.'"

Nessy looked at Flora.

And Nessy let go of her mother's hand and took Flora's hand instead.

Flora was the person who first called Vanessa "Nessy." And by the time summer reading club was over and kindergarten in her immediate future, Nessy was Nessy to everyone.

Because the girls were in different grades, as they grew, they did not see each other in school very much. But as often as they could, they played together on weekends.

So when Flora spent her first night in the rented white house with the "as good as old" things her father had bought for her, Nessy was there with her.

They read Nancy Drew books, and they painted stars on their toes, and they made pizza from a box with Forster Smallwood's help. Then everyone watched a Laurel and Hardy show and ate popcorn.

Nessy slept next to Flora that night in the new little bed in the new room. And she gave Flora, that night, balance.

5

Yury often accompanied Flora into Wings and a Chair Used Books to see what was new in the Young People's Nook. Miss Meriwether was very proud of her selection of used books for young readers, especially those books she called "extra vintage." Flora had read several extra-vintage books about a child named Honey Bunch, and many about a girl named Meg, and she was planning soon to dive into *The Boy Allies*.

When Yury stopped into the store with her this Monday afternoon, they decided to read a book out loud to each other, taking turns with the chapters.

It wasn't easy to settle upon a title. Flora was sure that Yury would enjoy *Meg and the Disappearing Diamonds*, but he wasn't that sure. Yury was positive they both would love a book about tigers called *Man-Eaters of Kumaon*, but Flora was positive they both would not.

Finally they settled on a very worn book that had on its cover a drawing of a boy and a girl who appeared to be spying on an oil well. It was called *Nora Force at Raven Rock*.

Flora and Yury were curious about a mystery that involved oil. And when they saw the title of the first chapter—"An Arrival and a Robbery"—they were hooked.

They took turns reading the book aloud, Yury sitting cross-legged on the floor beside the velveteen chair. They kept their voices low in case a customer came in, but on this day the store was empty, and Flora's mother was in the back wrapping some books to mail.

The two of them shared Nora's adventures to the middle of chapter 3—"Happy Landings!"—when Nora's airplane ride created something of a diversion.

"Right into the vortex of the storm headed the airplane," Yury read aloud.

"Does 'vortex' mean a tornado?" Flora interrupted.

Yury thumbed ahead.

"I don't think it's a tornado here," he answered. "This part has a girl leaving the plane, safe and sound."

"Good," said Flora.

"Yes," said Yury. "Surely an airplane would be the worst place to be in a tornado."

"Definitely," agreed Flora.

Both Flora and Yury worried quite a lot about tornados, although a tornado had never come to Rosetown. Still, there was always a possibility, and the two of them had made a joint disaster plan. It involved meeting up at the bookshop exactly three hours after the tornado landed.

They had decided against meeting at the doctor's office, since Yury's father might be very busy helping people. And they had decided against meeting at either of their homes, because Flora could not predict whether she would be at the yellow house or the white house when disaster struck. And besides, neither wanted to be the one sitting and waiting for the other to show up. Action was everything.

They read on. And when someone in the story said to Nora, *"Buck up, Nora Force,"* they both laughed.

"I'm going to say that to myself every time I worry about a test," said Flora. "Buck up, Nora Force!"

She was about to say more, when suddenly she saw, just out of the corner of her eye, a white fluffy tail, with a tip of yellow on the end, slide under the steps of Southwell's Barbershop across the street.

"What was that?" she said.

"What?" asked Yury.

"Something went under Mr. Southwell's front steps," Flora said. "I think it was a cat."

Nora Force and her troubles were completely forgotten now.

Flora and Yury crossed the street to have a look. It was dark beneath the porch steps, and neither could see anything at all there. Yet they both felt that something was looking back at them.

"I hope we aren't imagining this just because we've been reading a mystery," said Yury.

Flora didn't think so. She stared into the darkness with the same feeling she'd had a few weeks earlier in the farmlands: *expectation*.

They both assumed it was a cat there, watching them, but nothing moved.

Still, Yury thought he might have heard purring.

"Unless I am delusional," he said. "My father says that sometimes I am a master of grand delusion."

Flora smiled. She was glad to have a friend capable of grand delusions.

"We'll see you later," she said softly to the listener under the steps as finally, reluctantly, they walked away. "See you later."

6

Flora thought constantly about the cat with the white tail (and yellow tip) the next day. She even asked the principal of her school if she could come into the office during lunch and phone Miss Meriwether to find out if anyone had seen the cat. It was a bold act to ask the principal for such a favor. But Flora did.

"Not yet, Flora," said Miss Meriwether on the phone. "But we are all watching from our posts. I told the shopkeepers on this side of the street and those on the other side to call me the moment anyone sees a fluffy white tail going past."

She paused.

"With a cat attached," she added.

"Thank you," Flora said. "It means a lot to me."

"I know," said Miss Meriwether. "Don't worry."

But Flora did worry. All day at school she worried, and she missed two arithmetic questions because of it. Fourth-grade arithmetic was another matter that was very different from third grade. It seemed to require a person to think faster. Fast thinking was not Flora's strength, even without a cat to worry about. She wasn't as up in the clouds as her father could be, but she did like to take her time and carefully consider a thing, turn it about inside her head. Not a chance for that in fourth-grade arithmetic, where one had to pounce on the answer.

This being a Tuesday, after school Flora walked to her father's house, which was in the opposite direction of Southwell's Barbershop, where she really wanted to be headed.

Her father was making cinnamon toast when she arrived. He saw the look on her face.

"We will walk over there together after some toast, okay?" he said.

"Where?" asked Flora.

"You know where," said her father, smiling. "Your mother called me about Miss Fluffy Tail."

Flora put her books down and gave him a hug.

"I know she's there somewhere," Flora said.

"She could be a he," said her father, putting into the oven a pan of thick slices of bread laden with butter, sugar, and cinnamon.

"Mr. Fluffy Tail then," said Flora.

Flora's father handed her a tall glass of milk.

"Yury is as anxious as I am," Flora said. "He is probably drinking cups and cups of Mo's 24."

"When you finish up your snack, we'll go," said her father.

Soon the two were walking over to Main Street. They approached the bookshop to check in first with Miss Meriwether. But as they neared the door of the shop, Flora suddenly stopped.

She grabbed her father's sleeve and pointed to the shop window.

There inside Wings and a Chair Used Books, sitting on the purple velveteen chair, was a large white cat with a yellow tip on its fluffy tail, looking through the glass at Flora and her father.

"Miss Fluffy Tail," Flora whispered.

She walked softly into the shop, afraid to say anything lest the cat run away.

An empty can of tuna sat beside the cash register.

"She isn't wild," said Miss Meriwether, coming toward them from the Mystery Alcove. "Just a little sensitive, I think."

Miss Meriwether smiled at Flora.

"You two should get along splendidly," she said.

7

Flora's mother, Emma Jean, had been planning to be an English teacher when she met and married Flora's father, Forster. And Forster had been planning to take photographs of America and publish them in a book when he met and married Emma Jean.

Then, before Emma Jean could finish her studies and before Forster could travel across America, they had a baby daughter whom they named Flora. And raising her became for them the plan that mattered most.

Flora knew that her mother worked three after-noons a week at Wings and a Chair Used Books because it put her "in touch with paper." That is how her mother described it. Holding books and seeing the printed black ink on the pages made her mother happy. She felt useful, her mother said. Useful to the books.

Emma Jean Smallwood loved poetry best, and when she and Flora went to the Windy Day Diner or to the Peaceable Buns Bakery, Emma Jean often had a book of poems tucked inside her bag, which she sometimes pulled out to read to Flora. Flora had been listening to poems since she was a baby.

So when the white cat with the fluffy tail came to the bookshop to sit on the velveteen chair, and when the next day it followed Flora all the way home, Flora's mother told her to be thoughtful when choosing a name for her new companion.

"Think about the sound of the name," Flora's mother said. "And whether you would want to hear that sound day after day, if you were a cat."

Flora chose "Serenity."

She liked the soft *S* sound that began the name. And she liked the "tea" sound at the end of the name because it reminded her of Mo's 24 and her friend Yury.

Flora had hesitated to adopt Serenity (who was clearly a stray, for she had many fleas and was thin) until Flora first asked Yury if he would like to adopt the cat for his own. Yury had said good-bye to his old cat, and Flora worried that he might need a white cat with a fluffy tail much more than she did.

So she called him to ask whether he might need the cat for his own.

Flora did not ask Yury if he *wanted* the cat. That might have sounded cold, as if she herself did not want it. And she really wanted it with all her heart. She asked if he needed the cat.

And Yury's reply was this:

"Thank you for asking. But it's you she came looking for."

Flora wanted to cry when Yury said this. It is a rare thing when a friend wants, really wants, you to be happy.

"She has some fleas," was all Flora could manage to say.

Thereafter, things were very different in the yellow house, with a cat sleeping on the back of the sofa, or on top of the piano, or in the basket in the broom closet. And when Flora went to the white house five streets over, things were very different there, too. For Serenity always came along.

When Nessy spent the night, the girls made room for the cat between them.

Flora worried, though, about Yury not having a pet. But shortly after Serenity arrived, Yury told Flora on their walk after school that one of his father's patients had a puppy left from a litter of collies. And Yury's father and mother had said that the puppy could be his.

"Oh, that's wonderful!" said Flora. "Have you thought about a name?"

"Yes," said Yury. "I've whittled the list down to one hundred."

Flora smiled.

"And this will be your very first dog," she said.

Yury nodded.

"My father took Laurence to dog school," said Flora.

"Really?" said Yury.

"If you take your collie to dog school, could I come along?" Flora asked.

"Definitely," said Yury.

So Yury would soon have a puppy to raise. And Flora had found Serenity.

Flora thought, maybe things really were mostly right with the world. There were extra-vintage books to read, pizzas from a box to bake, poems and photographs to think about, a white cat sleeping on the back of the sofa. And the brown earth still met the blue sky at the horizon.

Fourth grade would have its challenges.

But all would probably be well. Especially because dog school was maybe just around the corner.

8

Rosetown seemed to have more than its share of good dogs, and this likely was because many of them were graduates of the Good Manners for Good Dogs dog school located at the back of Rosetown Hardware.

It was a useful combination—a dog school attached to a hardware store—because nearly every plumber and house painter in town (who were regular customers of the hardware) had a dog sitting in the front seat of his truck. And such a dog would need good manners indeed, to wait patiently as its owner went about his daily work with wrench or paintbrush in hand. Dogs in work trucks were so common that some people who did not have a dog at all still kept a bag of dog treats in the freezer just in case one showed up in response to a clogged drain.

And it was at the Good Manners for Good Dogs dog school where Flora and Yury were now found every Saturday afternoon for puppy class. They met in front of the hardware store every Saturday at two o'clock, then went around together to the back. They had attended three puppy classes so far, and all had been a great success.

Flora watched as Yury and his puppy—whose name was Friday—circled the large room with the rest of the puppies and their owners. She felt a warm happiness as she looked on, and she also felt proud of her friend. Yury, being new and from the Ukraine, might not have fit in so well with the residents of Rosetown. But he was fitting in beautifully.

When Yury adopted his puppy, his after-school schedule had changed because Yury took pet care very seriously. Now there was a puppy at home, restlessly awaiting his arrival from school so that the puppy could have a hearty run in the backyard and all of the tummy scratching that followed. Therefore, Yury's visits to his father's office were now shorter, and his time with Flora at the bookstore now barely ten minutes before he had to move on.

But they had Saturday afternoons. "Saturdays with Friday," as Flora put it.

Now it would be the fourth Saturday meeting of puppy class at Good Manners for Good Dogs. Yury was quite proud of Friday's progress thus far. The puppy had not once soiled the shiny linoleum floor of the training room. And Friday also did not try to sleep through the important parts of the class, as some of the other puppies did. Friday was very alert, always listening, always watching, and well on his way to becoming a dog with exceptionally good manners.

Flora would clap her hands softly whenever Friday did something right. Yury smiled at her after he gave Friday a mini-biscuit as reward.

And when the class time was over, everyone got to play! All of the puppies were let off their leads, and Friday and his friends chased and tumbled and played their puppy hearts out as their proud owners watched and laughed.

Yury stood with Flora as Friday rolled around with a puppy named Flash.

"I feel like a Little League dad," said Yury.

Flora smiled.

When Friday finally played himself almost to exhaustion, Yury picked him up in his arms. Then Yury and Flora and a sleepy puppy went around to the front of the hardware store to say good-bye.

Flora petted Friday's head.

"When Friday is a really good dog, he can meet Serenity," she said.

"Yes," said Yury.

They then went their separate ways. But as close friends often do, each turned around once, to check on the other, before turning the corner for home.

9

With her cat Serenity, Flora continued to travel
back and forth between the two houses she now
called home, making life "a bit floaty," as she once
described it. But everyone was managing, and there
seemed still to be much good will among everyone.
Flora's father said that this arrangement was a
chance for him and Flora's mother to adjust their
perspectives.

"What is 'adjusting perspective'?" Flora asked.

"Looking at something from a new angle," her
father answered.

"Like the way you move from one side of the street to the other when you're taking a photograph of a fender bender?" asked Flora.

"Exactly," said her father. "And 'fender bender' is a very apt comparison, by the way."

So the Smallwoods were all adjusting their perspectives, and so far it was going well. Forster had taken up oil painting, Emma Jean was learning to knit, and Flora was passing fourth-grade arithmetic.

What Flora always most enjoyed, everyone knew, was sitting after school in the purple velveteen chair. She loved Miss Meriwether's extra-vintage books, especially the writing in so many of them.

She often shared some of her favorite passages with her mother when they had sandwiches at the Windy Day Diner.

On this day, Flora opened up a slender old book called *Stories for Children* that had been inscribed, *To Christopher, Christmas 1929*.

"Nineteen twenty-nine," Flora said to her mother. "Not even you were born then."

Flora's mother smiled. "I was not yet even a possibility," she said.

"It's 1972 now," said Flora, "so Christopher is maybe . . ."

Flora took a few moments to calculate. "He is maybe a grandfather today," she concluded.

"That would be nice," said her mother.

Flora turned a page carefully. The book felt delicate in her hands, like a slender blade of grass.

"This is a good opening to a story," said Flora.

She read:

"Near the road is a snug little farmhouse called Home. In this cozy little house with its white window-frames, snug front porch, and well-kept walks, there lives a thrifty and happy family."

Flora's mother smiled. "I love 'thrifty,'" she said.

"So do I," said Flora. She and her mother were alike that way: they both loved good words.

The two ate their food in contented silence for a while, watching people in the diner come and go.

Then Flora's mother said, "What would you think about piano lessons?"

"For you?" asked Flora.

"No, sweetheart, for you," her mother answered, smiling.

Flora took a deep breath, as she always did before making a major decision. Her eyes scanned the farthest corner of the room. (She always did this as well.)

Then she looked back at her mother.

"Can Nessy take them, too?" Flora asked.

"Let's find out," said Flora's mother. "I'll call her mother tonight."

Flora nodded. She wanted to be careful not to feel too much happy anticipation, just in case she was disappointed if Nessy's mother said no.

Still, Flora felt that just-off-the-ground lightness when something lovely might be about to happen.

She realized that she had always wanted to play the piano. She just had not known this about herself until now.

10

Rosetown's only music store was called Four-Part Harmony, and it was a very popular place. The store had been operating in Rosetown since 1960, and in its early days it had mostly supplied band instruments to high school students and an occasional guitar to someone who loved Elvis.

But in recent years it seemed that everyone wanted to be a performer. The 1960s had been a time of great self-expression, with its make-peace-not-war hippies and their creative blossoming. And music had blossomed along with them. This was very good for Four-Part Harmony. Many new customers came into the store, looking for ways to express themselves. With the extra money he made, the store's owner, Mr. Teller, remodeled the back of the building to create a large new space with rooms for personal music lessons and also a performance room. He called this section of the store Part Five.

On Tuesday after school Four-Part Harmony was the destination of Flora and her friend Nessy. They arrived at the store accompanied by Flora's father, who had just finished taking photographs of the high school marching band.

"I am afloat in musical instruments today," Forster Smallwood said as he held open the door of the store for the girls.

Flora and Nessy barely heard him. They both were nervous, feeling shy, and they each grabbed the other's hand as they stepped into the building.

It is beautiful, thought Flora when she looked around the showroom.

Mr. Teller had arranged all of the stringed

instruments in one section of the showroom, and all of the brass instruments in another section, and the pianos and percussion in another. An exquisite cello sat glistening in its stand beneath soft lights, and the keys on every piano were shiny and white.

In a separate alcove there must have been one hundred or more guitars, electric guitars in bright metallic colors and folk guitars in warm wood. A few young men were trying out some of the guitars, and one young man in particular was quite a good guitarist. His fingers were quick and sure as they moved over the strings, and Flora felt a sudden upwelling of feeling inside her in response to the beauty of his music.

Flora squeezed Nessy's hand to reassure her that everything was good.

Flora's father introduced the girls to Mr. Teller, who was standing behind a glass case filled with packages of strings for every variety of stringed instrument. Mr. Teller welcomed them to the store and told them that each girl would have her own piano teacher in her own room in Part Five.

He gave Nessy a friendly smile.

"You are Vanessa?" he asked, reading the application in his hand, which had been completed by her mother.

"*Nessy,*" said Flora and Nessy together.

"Nessy," Mr. Teller repeated. "Well, Nessy, your teacher's name is Miss Larsson, and she is waiting for you in Part Five in room 1."

So many numbers, thought Flora.

Nessy nodded and squeezed Flora's hand again.

Then Mr. Teller looked at Flora.

"And you are Flora," he said. "Your teacher will be with you as soon as he finishes with his customer over there."

Mr. Teller pointed toward the young men standing among the guitars.

Flora looked at her father, her eyes wide.

Flora's father smiled at her. Then he asked Mr. Teller which of the young men was Flora's teacher.

Mr. Teller then pointed to the young man who had just made the guitar sing so beautifully.

"That one there in the corduroy jacket," said Mr.

Teller. "His name is Zachary, and he is our musical genius."

Flora's father then looked at her with his own wide eyes.

"Maybe a future rock star," he said.

Flora was so surprised. She had been certain her piano teacher would be a gray-haired man with a pair of wire spectacles perched on the end of his nose.

Nessy looked at Flora.

"Groovy," said Nessy.

Mr. Teller and Flora's father laughed. The girls laughed too.

Four-Part Harmony was a whole new world—in Rosetown!

11

All good things go by threes, wrote the wise author of *Stories for Children.*

Flora had been pondering this idea as she helped her father plant a row of winter kale in the empty window boxes of the white house. Serenity was sleeping inside in her little cat bed, as the November day was blustery and the kitchen so warm.

"Do good things go by threes?" Flora asked her father as she scooped potting soil from a bag.

Her father paused in his planting. He nodded his head.

"I have heard that," he said, "although I have also heard that bad things go by threes."

"Well, that would be unfair," said Flora. She did not want any bad thing to happen at all, but that two more bad things might be promised to follow was too much to even consider.

"Maybe it is only mildly bad things," said her father.

Mildly bad, thought Flora.

"I guess that could be," she said. "But I am hoping good things go by threes and bad things only by ones."

"So am I," answered her father.

Flora looked closely at her father, Forster Smallwood, at his tall thin frame in the red flannel shirt and canvas dungarees, at the lock of hair that always fell across his glasses. Today his face was ruddy, but sometimes his face was gray with worry. Flora knew that Rosetown was the best place for someone like her father, someone who felt so keenly all the things wrong with the world. A noisy city would never do.

"Nessy and I have a piano recital in two weeks," said Flora.

"Really?" said her father, his eyes brightening.

"Zachary is working on my posture," Flora said. "I slump."

"Probably from sitting for hours in a certain bookshop chair," said her father. "Are you looking forward to the recital?"

Flora nodded.

"I am," she said. "And Nessy is really going to wow them."

Nessy had discovered that she had a talent for piano. At least, Nessy's piano teacher Miss Larsson had discovered this. Nessy did not know what was good or bad in music. She just played.

When she had visited Flora in the yellow house recently, Nessy sat down at Flora's piano and played a series of difficult scales by heart. By heart!

"I am barely past Every Good Boy Does Fine," Flora said to her friend. "You are amazing, Nessy!"

Nessy was so pleased to be good at something. She had been looking, hoping, for an activity that felt all her own, and mattered, just as Flora had found in reading the dear old books at Miss Meriwether's bookshop. Nessy needed something thoroughly Nessy.

But until the piano, nothing had been a good fit. Nessy's mother had sent her to classes for tap dancing, for swimming, for roller-skating, and for volleyball. But all of these had just caused Nessy to bite her nails and lose sleep.

Why her mother had never considered piano lessons was unclear. Perhaps Nessy's mother thought that group activities were best.

But then Flora's mother opened the door to piano lessons. She had wanted them for Flora. And Flora wanted them for Nessy.

Because of this, Nessy now belonged to something. She belonged to the piano.

The recital was to be on a Saturday morning at ten o'clock. The time fit nicely with Flora's schedule, for she always had something very important to do Saturday afternoons at Rosetown Hardware.

"Can you come to my recital in the morning

before puppy class?" Flora asked Yury on their walk from school to downtown.

"Of course," said Yury. "I will practice shouting 'Bravo' until then."

"You can meet Zachary," said Flora. "He is, as my father put it, a hard taskmaster. Which means he won't let me have a lazy mind or lazy fingers. Don't let Zachary's long hair and Rolling Stones T-shirt fool you: he is a perfectionist."

"Then you will be perfect," said Yury.

"Oh, no," said Flora. "I like playing piano, but I am not very good at it. Zachary could do so much better if Nessy were his student."

"I disagree," said Yury. "How many other piano students can quote lines from old books?"

"Do you want to hear my favorite for this week?" Flora asked.

"I'm ready," said Yury.

Flora stopped and straightened her shoulders.

"The first ice of the season lay as smooth as glass across the river."

She waited.

"Very nice," said Yury.

"It's from *Stories for Children*," said Flora. "1929."

"I can see it in my mind," Yury said.

"What a lot of people don't know is that words are music too," said Flora.

Flora and Yury arrived at Wings and a Chair and stopped to take a look at the new display in the window before Yury went on to his father's office and then home to Friday.

"Look," said Yury. "There's a book called *Foraging for Wild Edibles*."

Flora and Yury, survivalists to the bone, looked at each other then raced for the door.

12

Forster and Emma Jean Smallwood were like many other young parents in America. They had come through a time when their country was darkened by war, assassinations, riots, and often a loss of hope.

Yet Forster and Emma Jean shared a real sense of purpose for their lives. When they found out they would be having a child, they decided to move to a place in Indiana where they hoped life would be simple: Rosetown.

Sweetly, everything really felt simple and easy, at first. After their baby, Flora, was born, each morning one of them would put her in the baby carriage and take her to the central park, placing her in one of the baby swings and swinging her gently, singing old folk songs to make her smile. Forster and Emma Jean had faith that if they stayed in Rosetown, life would always make sense to them.

And yet today they were more confused than they ever had been, and were now living five streets apart while Flora navigated the distance between them.

Though at first their separation had made Flora deeply sad, the situation was not now as uncomfortable as it had been. Some months had passed since her father carried linens and silverware five streets over, and there was a feeling now of a kind of relief. As though a wind had blown through the family and loosened something that had been stuck.

Flora observed other children's parents, who managed to live in the same house, together, and who seemed to do all the things expected of them. They looked like they were winning the contest for best parents.

But Flora knew, she just knew, that her father and her mother were very special people, and she was glad to be their daughter, even if they did not do the expected things.

So when the exciting day arrived, it was a natural and easy thing for Forster Smallwood to walk from the white house five streets over to the yellow house and slide his long thin body into the front seat of the family station wagon to ride with his wife, Emma Jean, and their beloved daughter, Flora, to her first piano recital.

Flora's mother had helped her find a new dress for the event, one with a blue satin sash, and they dyed a pair of white flats the same shade of blue, and Emma Jean plaited Flora's hair into a long braid, which she tied with a blue ribbon.

Being her reflective father's daughter, Flora had a tender feeling for the passing of time as she rode to the recital. She looked out the window at Rosetown, and she knew that days such as this would always be remembered, when she was older and everything was different.

It was all right, though. This reflection meant only that she appreciated what she had in her life.

When they arrived at Four-Part Harmony, a sign with blue lettering was posted on the door, welcoming everyone to the piano recital at ten o'clock in the performance room.

"The letters match my sash," Flora said to her mother as they walked inside.

"I noticed," said her mother.

They went inside and saw rows of folding chairs, many with people already seated in them, and a Baldwin piano in front. Mr. Teller's wife was serving as usher, and she handed Flora and her parents each a recital program.

Flora looked for Yury, but he hadn't yet arrived. Nessy was already seated with her parents and her older brother. Nessy was dressed all in white ruffles, and she looked like an angel.

"Good luck!" Flora whispered as she moved past Nessy's chair.

"You too!" Nessy answered.

And soon the recital began. First, each of the

four piano teachers stood before the audience and said a few words about teaching their students. Zachary was wearing a very hip black jacket and shiny black boots. Flora was quite proud to be one of his students, especially when he used the word "transcendent" in his talk. He winked at her when he sat down.

Then one by one the students went up to the piano, sheet music in hand, to play their pieces. The beginners went first, and this meant Flora.

When it was her turn, she stood up and looked behind her for Yury. And there he was in the last row, his large eyes behind his round glasses looking right at her. Beside him sat a man with the same kind of eyes and similar glasses, and Flora realized that Yury had brought his father along.

She waved, and Yury smiled, giving her the *okay* sign with his thumb and forefinger.

Flora played her piece—a Hungarian lullaby—just fine.

Nessy played her piece—a sonata by Beethoven—beautifully.

And for that hour when everyone was there in the hushed and respectful gathering, it was as if they all had stepped outside time. The young musicians—beginners, intermediate, and advanced—with their sashes and bow ties and carefully combed hair, all did their very best.

And everyone knew it was so.

13

Puppy class had been progressing very well. All of the puppies were now paying attention, even the ones who at first wanted to do nothing but roll on the floor and chew on someone's shoelaces. They all had learned to walk nicely around the room on lead and to watch their owners' faces after they came to a sudden stop. If the puppies did this, they each received a mini-biscuit. What the puppies were being prepared for was official dog school, when an understanding between owner and dog was everything. And it began with the eyes.

Yury also practiced often with his puppy, Friday, many times during the week. Between puppy practice, office duties, homework, and archery lessons, Yury had had little time to visit with Flora at Wings and a Chair. They both missed it.

Then, on the Thursday following Flora's recital, a mildly bad thing happened, followed by two more mildly bad things, and Flora found herself on the other end of Friday's lead in puppy class.

The events all took place during Yury's after-school visit to his father's medical office.

While Yury was preparing a pot of Mo's 24 tea for everyone, a woman in the waiting room suddenly could not find her eyeglasses and was upset that she could not read the movie star magazine she had picked up off the table.

The second mildly bad event happened immediately after that, for in her search among the chairs for her eyeglasses, she knocked over a floor lamp, which knocked over an asparagus fern, scattering dirt all over the carpet.

The receptionist at the desk then called out for

Yury to assist in all of the chaos, and that precipitated the third mildly bad thing to happen.

The receptionist was a highly excitable woman whose voice became quite shrill when such things as floor lamps and asparagus ferns went flying.

And her shrill *"Yury!"* gave Yury such a start, just as he was on his way with the tea tray, that he upset the tray, overturned the teapot, slipped on the wet mess he'd made, and badly—not mildly, actually—sprained his left arm.

A doctor's office is a perfect place to sprain an arm, if a person is bound to do so, and in no time at all Yury's arm was iced, then nicely wrapped in a sling. The asparagus fern was put back into its pot and the floor lamp righted. And the woman's eyeglasses were found, and when her appointment was finished, she went home carrying the movie star magazine that Yury's father had given her to keep as her own.

So all in all, the mildly bad things that had arrived by threes did not create too much disaster.

Except this: with his left arm in a sling, Yury

could not do puppy training exercises with Friday. For the left arm is essential in puppy training; it is on the owner's left side that a trained dog walks. The right arm of an owner is for supplying mini-biscuits.

Yury phoned Flora and explained his dilemma.

"Class is in two days," he said. "And it's puppy graduation! I won't be able to participate, and Friday won't receive his diploma."

"Of course he will receive his diploma," said Flora. "He just may not get an A."

"I don't think they give grades at puppy school," said Yury.

"I was kidding," said Flora.

"Oh," said Yury. He gave a small laugh. "Well, don't tell Friday. He's been working for an A!"

"Why don't we go to the class anyway," said Flora, "and I'll do the exercises with him."

"You mean out on the floor?" asked Yury.

"Sure," said Flora. "I've been watching you for weeks. I know what to do."

"Yes, you do," said Yury. "But Friday doesn't see

you as the boss. He thinks you are the professional head-scratcher."

"Let's try anyway," said Flora. "The worst that could happen is that Friday gets a C."

"They don't give grades at puppy school," said Yury. "Didn't you know that?"

They both laughed.

"Don't worry," said Flora.

"I'm going to worry," said Yury.

"Okay," said Flora.

So on Saturday, the eighth week of puppy class and a big day for all, Flora met Yury and Friday at the front of the hardware store. They walked around back to the dog school, where Yury bent down and kissed Friday on the nose before handing the lead over to Flora.

"Buck up, Nora Force," said Yury.

Flora smiled.

When owners and puppies arranged themselves around the room to begin, Friday looked up at the new person on the other end of his lead.

"Let's get an A," Flora said to him. "Friday: Sit."

Friday wagged his tail, then sat. Flora gave him a mini-biscuit, and they were off to the races.

The hour went by so quickly. All of the puppies exhibited lovely puppy manners, and each received a diploma and squeaky toy as commemoration for their hard work. Yury stood with Friday during the diploma presentation while Flora moved back into the audience of proud supporters. Yury's face was shining with happiness as he accepted the diploma for his good dog, Friday.

After class Flora and Yury and Friday walked to the Peaceable Buns Bakery. They found an empty bench outside, and Yury and Friday waited as Flora went inside. Soon she was back with a brown bag of cookies and an old crust of bread wrapped in a napkin.

The day was chilly, and winter was in the air.

"I feel snow in my nose," said Yury.

But both friends felt warm inside, as they shared life and a puppy on the sidewalks of Rosetown.

14

Snow had arrived in Rosetown in late November, to the delight of snow-lovers and also the owner of Mars Comics. The comic book business always fell off at the start of the school year, quite naturally, with the return of homework assignments, marching-band practice, and football games. But after the homecoming queen had been crowned and the final game played, the snow started falling and Mars Comics came back to life.

Flora was not a regular Mars customer, though Yury was. He owned many comics of which he was quite proud, most of which he had bought with the bit of money he earned helping his father at the office. Yury stored his comics in an old file cabinet and, unlike most other comics fans, could not bear to trade them, especially the Green Lantern, which was far and away his favorite.

And because Flora so loved vintage books, and was completely uninterested in comics, there was never any competition between them about reading materials.

Yury liked Mars Comics, but Flora *loved* Wings and a Chair Used Books. How lucky for her it was that Miss Meriwether no longer lived the life of a free spirit but instead had opened a shop. Flora watched Miss Meriwether move among the shelves in her long flowered skirts, and Flora hoped she might one day be as interesting and as brave. Flora did not know if she could ever leave Rosetown, for she felt she might be lonely if she ranged too far out in the world. She felt that it was good to wake up in the morning and know that the day ahead would contain all that was familiar and true. What if she moved to London and woke up without that feeling? Perhaps if she brought along a friend. Perhaps then the world would not seem unpredictable.

For now, Christmas was approaching, snow was falling, and the weather had turned quite chilly.

"Serenity sits by the stove warming her whiskers every morning," Flora told Yury over the phone. Both had finished their homework, and Yury was calling before his favorite television show, *Columbo*, came on.

"My father does the same," said Yury.

Flora laughed.

"Did Friday play in the snow today?" she asked.

"Endlessly," said Yury.

"What will your family do for Christmas?" asked Flora.

"We'll drive to the Russian Orthodox church in Indianapolis," said Yury. "But our Christmas comes earlier than your Christmas."

"Really?" asked Flora.

69

"Yes," said Yury.

"The words in your church, are they all in Russian?" asked Flora.

"Yes," said Yury.

"And you understand them?" Flora asked.

"I do," said Yury.

"I'm in the Christmas choir at my church," said Flora. "But I don't harmonize well."

"Says who?" asked Yury.

"The choir director," answered Flora.

"You'll get better," said Yury.

Flora was not so sure. She had so looked forward to being in the Christmas choir and was finally old enough to participate this year. But the choir director had chosen music far beyond Flora's ability to follow, so she was stumbling along in rehearsal and doing her best to harmonize without attracting too much attention.

When Flora's father had picked her up after a recent rehearsal, she had told him all this.

"Well, if it's too difficult, why not wait until you're older?" he asked.

"I can't wait," said Flora. "I'm inside the singing now."

"Inside the singing?" repeated her father.

"If I'm in the audience, I'm outside the singing," said Flora. "But if I'm in the choir, I'm inside the singing. It's like the difference between just looking at a bear and being a bear. I feel like I'm a bear now."

Flora's father smiled. "That is the best reason for being in a choir that I ever heard," he said.

"I knew you'd understand," said Flora.

Flora felt such peace this holiday season. Rosetown was so beautiful and alive. A tall evergreen in the central park glowed with strings of colored lights, and artificial snow had been sprayed on the windows of all the shops to frame displays of sleds and bicycles and elves and candy canes. Green wreaths hung on all the lampposts. Santa Claus was visiting with the little children at the park bandstand every Saturday between the hours of two and four. And Christmas bells played each evening in the old German church.

Flora even felt great hope that soon her family would all live together again in one house. In the meantime her father continued to be a very good father and photographer. And her mother continued to be a very good mother and part-time shopkeeper.

But those part-time hours were about to change.

15

"Nessy, you will not believe where Miss Meriwether is going," Flora said as she caught up with her friend on Monday just as Nessy was stepping onto the school bus for home.

"Where?" asked Nessy, nearly missing the step.

"Paris!" said Flora. "I'll call and tell you everything!"

Indeed, Miss Meriwether had, quite unexpectedly, sailed into the blue by way of a Pan Am jet bound for France. She had phoned Flora's mother on Sunday night and asked if Emma Jean could

mind the shop for several days so that Miss Meriwether might spread her wings.

"A friend has offered to put me up in the heart of
Paris," said Miss Meriwether. "How can I refuse?"

Emma Jean was quite encouraging and, in fact,
excited for this challenge during the busiest book-
buying time of the year.

So on Monday morning Emma Jean Smallwood
awoke much earlier than usual—four thirty—so
that she might arrive very early at the shop and
be well prepared to serve Rosetown's used book
buyers. She dropped off Flora at the white house
so that Flora's father could prepare her a good
breakfast and so that Emma Jean could be at Wings
and a Chair Used Books long before the usual nine
o'clock opening.

Of course, this opening of the doors would be
anything but "usual," for not only was it Christmas
season, but Miss Meriwether was at present somewhere near the Palace of Versailles.

After school Flora and Yury walked together to
the bookshop to see how everything was proceeding.

When they arrived, they found seven customers waiting in line not only to pay for their books but also to have them wrapped for Christmas giving. This part of solo proprietorship—the wrapping part—was proving to be somewhat overwhelming for Emma Jean, as it slowed things down considerably.

"Oh, Flora!" she said when she saw her daughter coming through the door. "You are just the person we all need!"

Emma Jean set Flora to wrapping right away on the broad table behind the sales counter. And as Flora took on this task, Yury was surprised to find himself serving as a consultant to the other buyers in the store. For there were a few customers, who had not yet made up their minds, staring at the shelves in the Young People's Nook, quite confused about what to buy for the children on their lists. The sight of a nine-year-old boy—who surely had a useful opinion about young people's books—was cause for great relief.

One woman approached Yury. She was holding

a book about bugs called *Straight Wings*. Yury had already read this book on one of his visits to the shop, so he was able to answer her questions.

"Will my eight-year-old nephew like this book?" was her first question.

"Oh yes," said Yury, "especially the part about crickets. Did you know that crickets sing more slowly when it is cold outside?"

"I did not," said the woman.

"And they stop singing entirely when it is freezing," said Yury, "which helps people know when to cover their tomato plants."

"Fascinating!" the woman said. "But this is such an old book, published in 1939. Maybe it is out-of-date for a modern eight-year-old boy?"

Yury shook his head.

"I am pretty sure that crickets have hardly changed at all since 1939," he said.

"I'll take it!" said the woman.

Yury assisted two more customers in choosing one western and one space adventure. Then these book buyers all joined the line at the counter.

Emma Jean saw what Yury had done, and she gave him a big smile.

Flora had not noticed Yury as bookseller, though, for her nose was buried in ribbons, tape, and Santa Claus wrapping paper. She lifted her head only to say good-bye as Yury called "Farewell" from the door. He was late to tea-making and had yet to take Friday for his afternoon walk.

Emma Jean and Flora worked busily all the rest of the afternoon, and when finally they turned the lock of the shop door at six o'clock to walk to the Windy Day Diner for dinner, they were both quite spent.

Each ordered a malted milk with their meal, as it seemed that nothing else would do for bookselling fatigue.

"Do you think we will survive the Christmas shopping season?" Flora's mother asked as they walked slowly home in the dark, the colorful lights of the shops guiding their way.

"Only if we drink plenty of malted milks," said Flora.

"I think so, too," answered Emma Jean. She was exhausted, but she was also pleased by how exhilarating her day had been. There was just something about being *in charge*.

Serenity greeted them at the front door, and after much affection and canned fish, the cat curled up between them on the sofa, and all three fell asleep in front of the television, *White Christmas* continuing on, its happy ending just around the corner.

16

Flora had never seen a gated community until the day when she and her father had given Nessy a ride home for the first time.

"Why is there a locked gate?" Flora had asked Nessy.

"My father says that it keeps out the burglars," Nessy answered.

"Not the climbing monkey burglars," said Flora.

Nessy laughed.

Flora first felt a little sorry for Nessy, having to live in a neighborhood behind a big locked gate.

But once inside the gate, the houses seemed as friendly as any other kinds of houses, with warm lamps in the windows and welcome plaques on the doors.

Yet Flora knew that she herself was a town person. She loved the old sidewalks of Rosetown with their tall old trees. A town person could never be happy in a neighborhood of small new trees like those in Nessy's gated community. It was the towering oaks and chestnuts of Rosetown that gave Flora a feeling of being really rooted.

But she did still love visiting Nessy's home behind the gate. And Flora thought that Nessy might even be a famous pianist one day, at which time Nessy could buy her own house.

But Nessy always said that she just wanted to be a gardener.

Yury could not attend the performance of Flora's Christmas choir, as he was obliged to visit with out-of-town friends of his family that evening. But Nessy wanted very much to attend, so Flora's mother invited Nessy to come to the concert with both her and Flora's father and to spend the night with Flora afterward.

Of course Nessy said yes.

Before they left for the concert, Flora showed Nessy the postcard Miss Meriwether had sent from Paris. The card was illustrated with a street map of the city, and small drawings on the map located important landmarks.

"There's the Eiffel Tower," said Flora.

"And the airport," said Nessy, pointing to an airplane north of the city.

"Miss Meriwether is there somewhere," said Flora, "in that big city. I wonder if they have Christmas lights, too."

"Probably," said Nessy. "Paris probably has everything."

The girls examined the other points of interest on the card, then turned it over to read Miss Meriwether's brief message—*Bonjour, mes amis!*—which Flora's mother had explained as "Hello, friends!"

The card made them all smile.

At the Congregational Church it was exciting for Flora to be in the downstairs rooms of the church with the other choir members, donning robes, finding places in line, smoothing out the choral book in her hand. Flora thought it seemed dreamlike. She knew that this was another memory she would fold away and take out again one day to look at.

She followed her fellow choir members onto the stage of the beautiful old church. The lights were low, candles glowed in every window, and red poinsettias in baskets lined the aisles. Flora could not see where her parents and Nessy were sitting, but she knew they were out there, somewhere.

And here she was, inside the singing. She did her best to harmonize. And even if she did not do it especially well, Flora still stood with her shoulders straight, and she sang up to the rafters of the old church and beyond:

"The first Noel the angel did say . . ."

17

On the day that Miss Meriwether was to return to Wings and a Chair Used Books—December 24—the residents of Rosetown, Indiana, awoke to eighteen inches of snow outside their windows. The forecast had been for only three inches, and all of the weather people at the local TV stations were calling one another that morning to frantically compare notes. But it was too late for that. They all had gotten it wrong, and the west wind had blown in a blizzard.

Indiana is a state accustomed to heavy snow, so

no one in town was panicking. Things would get off to a late start, and this late start might be a matter of hours or a matter of days, depending on where City Hall sent the plows. But if everyone just made themselves a nice cup of cocoa and settled in, Rosetown would again be moving.

This was all well and good for most people. But for Miss Meriwether, who was, on December 24, at the airport in Indianapolis with six bags of luggage and several pounds of Belgian chocolate, a snowfall of eighteen inches was a disaster. She had promised to be back in charge at Wings and a Chair Used Books so that Emma Jean Smallwood could have Christmas Eve off to wrap gifts, make fudge, and watch *Miracle on 34th Street* at the Lyceum with her daughter, Flora.

Instead Miss Meriwether would be spending who-knew-how-long in Concourse A, unable to fly out of Indianapolis due to *a major weather event*, which was announced by an airport employee wearing an antler hat.

This left Emma Jean trying to decide what to do

on the day before Christmas, a day when perhaps many Rosetown residents had "book" on their shopping list and would be happy to come through the door of Wings and a Chair if someone could just shovel a path to get there.

Flora liked to think that she was always prepared for a disaster, but it was really her friend Yury who had the better survival skills. Yury owned many books on survival.

So Flora phoned her friend as soon as she saw the eighteen inches of snow on the ground.

"Rosetown shoppers will never stay home on December 24," Flora told Yury. "They will ski to the shops if they have to. And my mother needs to open up for business."

"You have no cross-country skis?" asked Yury.

"No," said Flora.

"Let me check a book, and I'll call you back," he said.

In five minutes Yury called back.

"I can make snowshoes," he said. "I have instructions from Survivor Bob."

"Really?" asked Flora.

"I'll be over in less than an hour," Yury said.

Flora hung up the phone and walked into the kitchen.

"How do you feel about snowshoes?" she asked the only available proprietor of Wings and a Chair Used Books on the most important shopping day of the year.

"How soon can you get some?" answered her mother.

Just about an hour later they heard a knock on the door, and there was Yury, standing on what appeared to be giant pine boughs laced to his boots.

"Told you," he said, frosting up his glasses with his cold breath. "All I need is pine."

Flora pointed to the large evergreens in the yard.

"We have plenty of that," she said.

And by nine o'clock, just in time to open, Flora, Yury, and Emma Jean reached Wings and a Chair Used Books, courtesy of Survivor Bob.

Emma Jean unlocked the door, flipped the sign from CLOSED to OPEN, and within twenty minutes the first customer arrived on snowshoes, real ones. Yury went home to help his father knock ice off the eaves.

It was an amazing day at Wings and a Chair Used Books. Customer after customer arrived, unstrapping snowshoes or pairs of cross-country skis out front, then coming inside to find that book that had been "at the back of my mind for weeks," many explained.

And this is the story of any proudly owned used-book shop: that someone, at some time, has stumbled upon a kind of buried treasure within its shelves. But unlike shiny gold, which is taken instantly, this treasure—a vintage book—in a used-book shop is often left behind, to linger at the back of the mind for a while. Then there arrives the day when it becomes clear that that vintage book should belong to a certain someone. And this day of clarity is often December 24, which is why it was so important to Emma Jean Smallwood to turn over that sign and switch on the lights.

When Flora was not wrapping books for those

hardiest of Rosetown shoppers, she placed herself in the velveteen chair by the window and read *The Girl from Tim's Place*, 1906, inscribed to John L.:

It was a desperate chance—a foolhardy step—a journey so appalling, so almost hopeless, she might well hesitate.

Flora smiled as she read those words and wondered whether her mother might have had the same thoughts when Yury showed up at the front door wearing tree branches.

Flora looked out of the window at the shops across the street, where lights had been turned on and coffee set to brew.

It was Christmas Eve in Rosetown, and there was everywhere more hope than hesitation.

18

Miss Meriwether finally arrived in Rosetown on the day after Christmas, having traveled from Indianapolis by Greyhound bus. The Rosetown municipal airport was simply too small an enterprise to be up and running so soon after a big snowfall, so a bus was the only option.

Flora and her mother were quietly organizing the shelves in the store when Miss Meriwether finally blew in, carrying several boxes of chocolates and wearing a glamorous red velvet coat. Flora threw her arms around Miss Meriwether and welcomed her home.

"Emma Jean and Flora, I am so very sorry," said Miss Meriwether. "I hope I did not complicate your Christmas too much."

"Oh, no," said Flora's mother, giving Miss Meriwether a warm hug. "We had many adventures we would not have had otherwise."

"Thank heaven," said Miss Meriwether.

"Thank Yury," said Flora.

"What, dear?" asked Miss Meriwether.

"I'll explain later," said Flora.

"Well, I brought enough chocolates to feed an elephant," said Miss Meriwether. "And speaking of elephants . . ."

She reached into her bag and withdrew a small silver box. She handed the box to Flora.

"For you," said Miss Meriwether. "Something to wear until you can do your own shopping in the flea markets of Paris."

Flora caught her breath. She had not expected anything from Paris for herself.

She opened the box. Inside lay a delicate silver chain holding one very small charm: an elephant.

"Elephants are special," said Miss Meriwether.

"That is what Yury always says," said Flora. "Thank you very much."

She lifted the necklace from the box. It felt much too important to wear.

"Is it all right if I save it for a special occasion?" asked Flora. "It's so beautiful."

Miss Meriwether smiled.

"Of course, dear," she said. "And there are sure to be many."

So things at the bookshop returned to normal. Emma Jean went back to three afternoons a week. And the streets of Rosetown were all plowed, the sidewalks shoveled, and, after New Year's Day, the colored lights and green wreaths were taken down, stored away until next Christmas.

During the holiday break from school, Yury helped his father with some light maintenance at the office, between cups of Mo's 24, and he walked Friday to the central park to make new dog friends. Yury was very protective of Friday, and he never let the puppy off lead when they were out and about, just as the instructor at Good Manners for Good Dogs had taught.

"All it takes is one squirrel," cautioned the instructor, "and away goes your dog."

Yury was determined that Friday would not go away. He kept Friday on lead and gave him mini-biscuits as reward for such good manners. Then when they got home and into the fenced yard, the lead clicked open and Friday ran a hundred circles in the snow.

For Flora, during the break, there were favorite board games to play when Nessy visited—Flora liked Clue and Nessy liked Candy Land—and there was time for Flora and her father to be together in his rented white house, watching old movies on television. And sometimes they walked to the camera store to look at special lenses and the European cameras her father said he could never afford but loved to admire. She admired them as well.

It was wonderful to have these long, empty winter days to fill up however she liked.

But Flora also looked forward to going back to

school, even in the snow, even in the ice, for she loved the old brick building, its radiators filling the rooms with heat, the aroma in the hallway of bread rolls baking in the school kitchen, the glistening shine of polished floors, and the reliable presence of pencils and chalk and large round globes.

A break was nice, but ordinary days were better.

19

February was hushed and cold. The nights were longer, so schoolchildren awoke in darkness and traveled to Rosetown Primary in darkness. They stomped their feet at the bus stop to stay warm, and when finally the headlights of the school bus appeared on the horizon, they applauded with their mitten-covered hands.

Flora was not a bus rider, so on these dark February mornings her parents took turns walking with her to school. Forster always brought along his camera. For the newspaper, Forster had taken hundreds of photographs of Rosetown citizens at hallmarks of their lives, but on his own time Forster brought along his camera and watched for what he called the "sublime moment."

A sublime moment was a split-second moment in time when suddenly something was revealed and then as suddenly gone. A swift making a perfect dive into the chimney of a grain factory; the blue flash of lightning inside a thunder cloud—those fleeting chances for a remarkable photograph, if Forster was there at the right time.

Because of her father's search for sublime moments, Flora tried to collect her own. Most of them involved her cat. Flora would see Serenity sitting in the window in the sun, and in her mind Flora would snap a photograph. Flora had a very large photo collection in her head, she once told her father.

He just smiled and said, "I'm sure."

Lately both of Flora's friends had something new to tell her. Nessy had said that she could not tell Flora her news until Flora came to her house on

Saturday, which was still three days away.

"You will be happy I made you wait," Nessy had said on the telephone. "You'll see."

Flora tried to imagine what Nessy might be waiting to tell her on Saturday, but the possibilities stretched all the way to the moon, so she gave up thinking about it.

Yury, on the other hand, had promised that he would tell Flora his news today on their walk after school to the bookstore. They had been working their way through the Walton Boys series. The three Walton brothers seemed always to be cast out in nature amid dire circumstances. Naturally this appealed to Flora and Yury. And they were hoping that no one would buy all of the titles until they finished the series.

Today on their walk to the store, both of them bundled in wool and flannel, Yury was eager to tell Flora his news.

"There is a Scrabble Club forming at Moonwalk Toys and Games," Yury said. "And my parents think that I should join for the mental challenge.

Ukrainians like mental challenges, they said. So I wondered if you would like to go with me."

"You mean to play Scrabble?" asked Flora.

"Yes," said Yury. "To join up and play."

"I can't," said Flora. "I am terrible at Scrabble.

"I like letters, and I like words," she continued. "Actually, I love words. But when they turn into objects on a board, my mind turns off."

"Really?" said Yury. "I guess that means no."

Flora pointed to the top of her head.

"Completely off," she said.

"Well, I think I will give it a go," said Yury.

"Of course you should," said Flora. "You'll win every game."

"Maybe not," said Yury. "The club is for ages nine to fourteen."

"Nine to fourteen?" repeated Flora. "I am positive now that I am not joining. Fourteen is ninth graders!"

"Yes," said Yury. "I must be crazy."

"You will be great," said Flora.

"You are saying that," said Yury, "but I don't think you mean it."

"Well," said Flora, "I might not one-hundred-percent mean it."

Yury laughed. "So much for encouragement!" he said.

They walked into Wings and a Chair and found the Walton Boys book they were halfway through: *The Walton Boys in Rapids Ahead,* published 1958.

"We left off when Bert was telling Howard to hang his shoes on a line to keep porcupines from eating them," said Yury.

Flora found the page and settled into the velveteen chair. Yury sat down on the floor beside her.

"Help me watch the clock," he said. "Fifteen minutes and I have to go."

"Okay," said Flora. She began reading aloud:

"'Well, suit yourself,' said Bert patiently. 'I just hope one of us wakes up in time if that porky comes along. . . .'"

20

By now Flora had grown quite used to living in both the yellow house and the white house, and although it was an unusual arrangement, this was, after all, the '70s, and people had become more experimental about life. Even in Rosetown.

Of late, her worrying father had become concerned about the environment and about the careless use of pesticides poisoning everything and everyone. Too much thinking about such matters could weigh him down, and he took long, solitary drives through the countryside to lift his spirits.

He always told Flora that the best medicine for the blues was a field of birds.

Flora's mother, more practical and more social, continued to love working in Wings and a Chair. She loved books of all kinds, and she also loved the art of bookmaking: the wonderful varieties of typeface, the feel of the paper, the cover design. Emma Jean treasured books.

From her parents Flora had gained an appreciation for the loveliness of life. And Rosetown itself—with its ornate Gothic and Italianate-style buildings, the gas lamps gracing City Hall, the fountain of angels in the town's central park—reflected what Flora's parents both hoped for the world: a kind of divine order.

Saturday eventually did arrive, and, as he had promised, Flora's father drove her to Nessy's house.

"I'll be back at three o'clock," her father said. "Be sure Nessy is ready to open the gate, or I may have to helicopter in."

Flora smiled, then went running up to Nessy's front door. She rang the bell, and when Nessy and her mother opened the door, they all waved good-bye to Flora's father and Flora stepped inside.

Nessy gave her a hug and helped her hang up her coat.

Nessy had that look that Flora knew so well, after years of friendship. It was the look that came just before Nessy spilled a secret she was bursting to tell.

"I have a pet!" said Nessy immediately. Her face was lit with joy.

"A *pet*?" asked Flora.

"I do!" said Nessy, taking Flora's hand. "Come and see!"

She led Flora toward the den, and when they stepped into the room, before Nessy could say anything more, Flora cried, "Oh! Oh! Oh!"

For there in a big beautiful cage sat a beautiful little bird.

"His name is Sunny," said Nessy proudly. "He is my canary."

The little yellow bird cocked his head to one side at the sound of Nessy's voice.

"He's listening to you," said Flora.

"I know," answered Nessy with a smile.

"Hello, Sunny," Flora said softly. The little bird hopped to a different perch in the cage and gave a small chirp.

Flora looked at the large cage.

"His home is so big," said Flora.

"It's so he can fly," explained Nessy. "Canaries need to fly."

"How did you get him?" asked Flora.

"Someone at the bank where my father works had to find a home for Sunny," said Nessy. "Sunny is too delicate to move to San Francisco."

"I agree," said Flora.

So it was Nessy's father who had brought the little canary and his enormous cage home to Nessy.

"My father didn't even ask my mother," said Nessy. "He just said to my mother that it was 'good for business and good for Vanessa.'"

Flora smiled.

"And Sunny *is*," said Flora. "Sunny *is* good for you!"

Nessy told Flora about all the ways she took care of Sunny.

"I clean his water bottle and give him fresh seed every day," said Nessy. "And I change his toys around so he doesn't become bored."

She pointed to a shallow bowl in the bottom of the cage.

"He takes his baths there," she said.

And she pointed to a piece of fabric folded under the table.

"That's the cloth I cover his cage with at the end of the day, as soon as the sky gets dark," said Nessy. "It helps him go to sleep."

Flora loved the image of the little yellow bird fast asleep in his dark, safe, covered home.

"He *loves* spinach," said Nessy.

"Yuck!" said both girls, laughing.

"And he likes oranges and cucumbers and broccoli and apples and so many good garden things," Nessy continued. "When I become a gardener, I'll make a little patch just for Sunny."

"Does he talk?" asked Flora.

"He *sings*!" said Nessy. "Watch."

She walked over to the piano and started playing. All at once Sunny lifted his small head and began singing, singing so beautifully that Flora felt she might cry.

Nessy stopped playing. Sunny flew around his cage to work off his excitement.

"Let's get some cucumbers for him in the kitchen," said Nessy.

"Let's!" answered Flora.

It was a very happy visit.

21

Fourth grade had been so much more difficult than third grade for Flora, and only now did she have some ground under her feet. It had taken her a long time to feel like a fourth grader and to realize that school would be a more serious business from now on. Flora was "not a natural scholar," said her mother, reminding Flora that she still had many other admirable qualities.

But there was one part of fourth grade Flora did love, and that was the Encyclopedia Hour.

Every week Flora's teacher, Mr. Cooper, had

started allowing the students to explore twenty-two volumes of the World Book Encyclopedia. The volumes were large and heavy and were arranged alphabetically on a shelf. It was a 1962 edition, and since this was 1973, Mr. Cooper apologized for not having a more up-to-date set. ("If I bought a new set every year," he said, "I couldn't afford to restore my old Chevy!")

Flora might browse the *A* volume one week, then jump to the *R* volume the next. The books were filled with all the information a person could ever want to know. And Flora was interested. She had not known until fourth grade and Mr. Cooper's Encyclopedia Hour that she was interested in the wider world. If all of fourth grade could be about the encyclopedia, Flora thought, school would be fine.

When Mr. Cooper introduced the Encyclopedia Hour, the first volume Flora reached for was *C*. Volume *C*, of course, would include "cat." She found "cat" in the large book, and an entire seven pages with photographs and drawings was devoted to cats. Flora loved the World Book Encyclopedia that instant.

Looking at the photographs, she determined that her cat, Serenity, might be a relative of the Ragdoll cat. The photograph of a Ragdoll cat looked very much like Serenity, although Serenity was a different color, being white with a yellow tip. Flora smiled at the name "Ragdoll." It was such a tender name.

The article was thick with useful and entertaining information. Flora enjoyed how it began with its observation that cats make faithful, friendly companions.

Yes! Serenity was as faithful and friendly as any pet could be. She followed Flora from room to room in her house, and the moment that Flora sat down, Serenity jumped into her lap. There were times when Flora put off doing important things—such as phoning Nessy when she said she would—because Serenity had just made herself perfectly comfortable in Flora's lap and Flora was reluctant to disturb her. Serenity closed her eyes and purred, and if Flora did not have a book at hand, she simply found things to think about.

The encyclopedia article cautioned that a cat's bed should never be in a drafty place or "a damp cold basement." Well, Flora could not imagine anyone putting a dear cat into a cold basement! And if a person absolutely had to do so, Flora hoped that at least sufficient wool and flannel would be provided! But avoiding the basement entirely was the best idea, and she was glad the encyclopedia agreed. Serenity had four warm beds in both of Flora's homes. In pleasant weather Serenity chose those beside the windows, and in cold weather she always chose the one nearest the stove.

The encyclopedia taught Flora much that she did not know about cats. She did not know, for example, that some cats turn on water faucets and take a drink. Serenity had not yet tried that trick.

The writer of the article seemed to understand cats thoroughly. When Flora read that "cats will often refuse to do something that might make them look silly," she was certain the writer must be a cat owner. Who else would know?

Encyclopedia Hour was never dull. Flora looked at illustrations of the human skeleton and at stories and photographs of important people like the nurse Florence Nightingale. She examined drawings of birds and submarines and the insides of a frog.

And one day Flora picked up the *U* volume, and she looked up "Ukraine." The article was not very long and there were no pictures, which was disappointing. She wanted to see what Yury's native country looked like.

The article described the Ukraine as a place that other countries wanted to control because of the valuable minerals in its ground. For a while the Ukraine would be taken over by one country, then another would take over, and then another. Its biggest city, Kiev, was the birthplace of the country of Russia, but Russia did not always stay in control of the Ukraine.

Flora wondered if this was why Yury's family left when he was six years old: to escape all of the troubles there.

So she asked him about it on their walk after school.

"My father was invited to teach for a year in Chicago," explained Yury, "so my family came to America. But when it was time for us to go home, there was too much conflict in our country, and my parents decided not to go back. My father finished teaching, and then he moved us here to Rosetown."

"It's sad that your family isn't able to go back home," said Flora. She knew that it would break her heart to leave Rosetown and never be able to come back.

"My mother is sad sometimes," said Yury. "She hasn't gotten used to when the sun rises here. She is sometimes still awake and asleep with the Ukrainian sun."

"Do you want to go back?" Flora asked.

"Someday I think I will," answered Yury. "To visit, at least. Imagine a place where there are thousands of Yurys! I will be just another boring Yury."

"Not boring," Flora said.

"You could come with me," said Yury. "We

could bring ice skates. It is very cold there."

Flora thought maybe she would, one day. Encyclopedia Hour had made the world seem so much smaller. As if she belonged to all of it.

22

The Scrabble Club at Moonwalk Toys and Games had met just three times when Yury decided it was not for him.

Flora was sitting with Yury and Friday in the town's central park one Sunday afternoon when Yury told her about his decision.

"I did pretty well, actually," Yury said. "I was a bingo winner more than once."

"Bingo?" asked Flora. "What?"

"In Scrabble," said Yury, "when a player makes a word with all seven tiles, it is called a bingo."

"Oh," Flora said. "No wonder I didn't know."

Yury smiled and continued his story.

"I was the youngest player there, of course," he said. "But I didn't mind. Scrabble is a calm game, so I was calm."

"Then what happened?" asked Flora.

"I began to turn into Wolf Man," said Yury.

Flora laughed.

"Wolf Man?" she repeated.

"I'm usually a mild-mannered person, right?" asked Yury.

"Right," said Flora.

"Well, Scrabble Club brought out the beast in me," said Yury. "I would actually lie awake at night thinking about how to prey on the other players' weaknesses so I could destroy them!"

"Wolf Man," said Flora.

"Precisely," said Yury.

Then he smiled.

"So I decided to take up bowling instead," he said.

"Bowling?" asked Flora. "There's a bowling club?"

"Well," answered Yury, "I guess my parents and I could call ourselves a club."

"Your parents are bowling, too?" asked Flora.

Yury nodded.

"We had our first bowl at Starlight Lanes yesterday," he said. "Every other game is free on Saturday mornings. And it was fun! I was a terrible bowler, and it was great!"

Flora laughed.

"I think we might even buy our own bowling shoes," said Yury.

"Amazing," said Flora.

The two friends sat awhile longer in the park, scratching Friday's head and talking of many things: their favorite Beatles songs, whether Mr. Cooper would take the class on a field trip in the spring, the possibility of life on other planets, and the new bubble-gum-flavor ice cream at the Sweet Shoppe.

It was a good Sunday afternoon. And Flora even had something good to look forward to on the following Sunday afternoon.

Miss Meriwether had promised to have Flora and Emma Jean to lunch at her apartment to thank them for taking care of the shop while she was in Paris. She knew that her trip had caused a bit of disruption to their Christmas. Miss Meriwether tried to live a cautious and deliberate life, but every now and then she just had to let loose and fly. So she wanted to thank them.

Flora did not really know Miss Meriwether very well outside of the bookshop. It was exciting to be invited for lunch.

So the next Sunday afternoon, Flora and her mother drove over to the blue Victorian house on Lincoln Street where Miss Meriwether rented an apartment on the second floor. The house was trimmed in white and had many stained-glass windows through which the warm interior lights glowed. A black wrought-iron fence made the house look all the more grand.

Miss Meriwether opened the door leading upstairs as soon as Flora and her mother stepped onto the porch.

"Welcome!" she said, and hugged them both. "Welcome to my *petit appartement*!"

Flora looked at her mother.

"Small apartment," her mother said, smiling.

They climbed the stairs and entered Miss Meriwether's home.

Flora took one look and loved it.

There were plants everywhere! On antique desks and tables and in large urns in corners and hanging in every window. And the plants were unlike any Flora had ever seen in a home.

"Your plants," said Flora, "they are so . . ."

"Eccentric!" said Miss Meriwether. "Like me!"

Miss Meriwether took Flora and her mother on a tour of her plants. Their names were as interesting as their shapes, names such as Elephant's Ear and Staghorn Fern and Paddle Plant. One large window was draped with a Passion Vine. And there was a miniature glass house sitting on an iron stand, and inside it were many lush ferns and mosses and orchids.

"This is a terrarium," said Miss Meriwether. "It is

always nice and moist in there, and I rarely have to add water."

"I saw a picture in a book of a big building that looked like this," said Flora, "and it was full of plants and even trees."

"That was a conservatory," said Miss Meriwether.

"I would love to visit one," Flora said.

"There is a conservatory in Indianapolis," said Miss Meriwether.

"Really?" asked Flora. She would tell Nessy. Maybe they could visit it together.

Miss Meriwether had the most interesting home Flora had ever seen. It looked just like the home of a free spirit. A line of square cloths with writing on them was hung across the top of the bay window, and these, Miss Meriwether explained, were prayer flags from Nepal, where she had once lived.

"The five colors represent the elements," she explained. "Blue for sky, white for wind, red for fire, green for water, and yellow for earth."

"So pretty," said Flora.

"In the Himalayas," said Miss Meriwether, "very

large prayer flags fly on the mountain passes, blowing prayers to the wind so that peace can spread to all people."

"I didn't know that," said Flora's mother.

Miss Meriwether had a very small kitchen with a very small table crammed into a corner, barely large enough for three people. An old cabinet with glass doors stood next to it, and its shelves were filled with many old tea tins and teapots. Flora read the names on some of the tins: *Black Dragon, Tippy South Cloud, Monkey King.* Being a word-lover, of course she enjoyed the unusual names.

When Flora and Emma Jean squeezed themselves into their chairs, Miss Meriwether revealed what had created the delicious aroma throughout the apartment: potato soup. She ladled the hot creamy chunks of potatoes and herbs into large pottery bowls. Then she sliced a fresh loaf of what she called Grainy Bread and placed the slices on the table beside a dish of rich butter.

"It is still winter in Indiana," said Miss Meriwether. "Soup is a must!"

The three had a wonderful lunch, and Miss Meriwether talked about whales and dolphins and how intelligent they are. She said they needed protection.

"I will protect them," said Flora.

"Good," said Miss Meriwether, smiling. "Good. You will do so much for the world, Flora, I just know that you will."

Dessert was a lovely rice pudding with raisins, served in small Japanese bowls with cups of oolong tea.

"The pudding is so good," said Flora.

"Thank you, dear," answered Miss Meriwether. "It is a recipe from an old yoga instructor during my limber years."

Flora smiled. She could just imagine Miss Meriwether standing on her head while her instructor cooked pudding.

At the end of their visit, Flora and Emma Jean thanked Miss Meriwether and promised to have her to their house when the tulips bloomed.

"I would love that," said Miss Meriwether. "And I can say hello to Miss Fluffy Tail," she added with a smile.

As Flora and her mother drove back home, Flora could still smell Miss Meriwether's potato soup, could still remember all the colors of the stained glass. She thought that she would like to have an apartment like that one day.

And she thought also about what Miss Meriwether had said concerning whales and dolphins, how Flora could help protect them. Here in Indiana, with farm fields spreading out in all directions, the world's oceans seemed so far away from her own small life.

But then she remembered the encyclopedia. And she told herself that she would choose the *O* volume next time, and find "ocean," and become better acquainted with its creatures.

Maybe one day she would travel far away and take a boat and meet some of them.

But always return to Rosetown.

23

Serenity the cat loved to sleep in the warm light of a sunbeam shining through window glass, and most especially in spring when all the birds had returned to Rosetown to entertain her. With the sound of birdsong coming from every tree, Serenity closed her eyes and purred with pleasure.

And because it was now spring, Flora had recently celebrated her tenth birthday. She was a bit unsettled to be at an age made up of two numbers instead of just one. Flora was not always receptive to change, and there was something in her that held on to the old, even to a single-number age, as nine had been. But she was adjusting to ten, and it helped that Nessy had also recently had a birthday, turning nine. If Nessy was always just right behind her, thought Flora, then surely things would not change too much. Flora could simply hand Nessy the age that Flora had been, like passing along an outgrown favorite coat. And they could adjust to the new numbers together.

Flora's need to hold on to the old probably had something to do with growing up in Rosetown, for very little changed, outwardly, there, and most people felt that this was a good thing. There were even old posts along the streets, here and there, that were meant for tying up a horse someone would ride to town. Many years had passed since someone had ridden a horse to the Rosetown Bank and Trust or to City Hall, but still most people could not part with the old hitching posts, so they remained. Flora was very much like those sorts of people.

And what better place, then, for her than a shop filled with old books? Wings and a Chair Used

Books had become very important to Yury, too. For when his family had left the Ukraine, they'd left behind all the old books of their own country. Reading vintage books with Flora had given Yury his own experience of memory and belonging. For with each book read, a spinner thread was sent out, connecting him to the past. He could always say to Flora, "Remember when the Mercer Boys rescued Colonel Morrell?" And Flora remembered with him.

One day on their walk Flora asked Yury whether he might become a doctor like his father.

"Oh, no," said Yury. "I would not have the patience."

"Patients?" repeated Flora. "Well, they would show up eventually."

"No," said Yury, smiling. "*Patience.* I do not have the patience to wait for results."

"Oh," said Flora. *"Patience."*

"My father says that the most important element of healing is time," said Yury. "He says that many people do not understand that time is their friend."

"I think it is," said Flora. She had always been a cautious person, and the more time she had to decide about a thing, the better she felt. Time was her friend.

"I am impatient," said Yury. "I would not be a good doctor."

"Well, what then?" asked Flora.

"I could rescue people," said Yury. "I could battle the elements to reach them on glaciers or out in the ocean."

"You could even train Friday to help," said Flora.

"That's it!" Yury said excitedly. "I will be a Search and Rescue person, and Friday will be my right-hand dog!"

It made sense to Flora. Even though Yury was very smart and could become a fine doctor, Flora could see that what Yury said was true: he needed to help people but without having to wait around.

"If you take Friday," she said, "you will need to teach him hand signals. The wind might be so loud that he wouldn't be able to hear you when you say 'stay.'"

"The advanced dog classes teach hand signals," said Yury.

He looked at Flora with happiness on his face.

"I believe I have just found my calling," he said.

"Probably," said Flora. "But first you have to pass fourth grade."

Yury looked at her and smiled.

"I can do that," he said.

24

There is something about spring that makes an unchanging thing suddenly seem changeable. Even Laurence's passing had been in spring, so he, too, must have felt the invitation to change. He had left the good earth a year ago, and what happened next for him no one could know, but they all hoped it would include pumpkin. Laurence had loved pumpkin.

But for Flora this spring, the unchanging thing that seemed ready to change was her parents' marriage.

For all these many months Flora and Serenity had

been going back and forth between the white house and the yellow house, and her parents had remained connected to each other in helpful and cooperative ways. But neither Forster nor Emma Jean had given Flora any hint that change might be in the stars. It was not until Flora's father began talking to her about that very thing—a change in the stars—that Flora realized something new was happening to her family.

In mid-April her father was driving her to visit Nessy, and they had been talking about their favorite foods, when Flora's father suddenly changed the subject.

"Has your teacher mentioned the April Lyrids by chance?" Flora's father asked her.

"Lyrids?" repeated Flora.

"Yes," said her father. "April Lyrids."

"No," said Flora. "What is an April Lyrid?"

"The Lyrids are meteor showers that happen every April," said her father. "Shooting stars, a lot of them. This might be a good year for seeing them in Indiana."

"Will we see them?" asked Flora.

"That is what I thought I'd ask you," said her father. "I thought maybe I'd drive you out to the countryside where the sky is darkest, and we could watch them for an hour."

"That sounds good," said Flora.

"And I thought I would ask Emma Jean to come with us," added her father.

"My mother Emma Jean?" asked Flora.

"I think she is probably the only Emma Jean we know so far," her father answered with a smile.

"Do you think she will want to come with us?" asked Flora.

"I am pretty sure she will," said her father.

Obviously changes had been happening right under Flora's nose.

She was silent a few moments.

Then she said, "That would be wonderful."

So wonderful that it made her worry that watching shooting stars with both her parents might not happen at all.

"Good," said her father.

They both were silent another few moments.

"The Lyrids are found in the constellation Lyra. They have been occurring for more than two thousand years," her father finally said.

"Two thousand," repeated Flora.

"More than," said her father.

"And people can wish on them, right?" asked Flora.

"Yes," said her father. "People can wish on shooting stars."

They arrived at the big gate, and soon they were pulling up in front of Nessy's pretty brick house. Nessy and her mother opened the front door and waved to them.

"So just let me know when," Flora said as she got out of the car. "About the stars."

"Definitely," said her father.

Flora ran up to Nessy at the door.

"I can't believe it," said Flora. "My parents and I are going on a date!"

25

It was the following Monday when Flora's teacher, Mr. Cooper, asked if he might speak with her for a few minutes after school. Naturally she said yes, and naturally she thought that she must be in trouble. Unlike some other children she saw who broke rules so easily that it seemed they were born to break them, Flora tried to follow rules to the letter. This was in part due to conscience, but it was also the result of being sensitive. She just could not bear the thought of being singled out for discipline. She might shatter like a piece of glass.

So for the rest of the hour until the final bell rang, Flora was so anxious that she could think of nothing else except what she might have done wrong. She missed everything Mr. Cooper said about the rain forest and about the homework assignment on the subject. Flora wondered if she was having something she had heard about called an out-of-body experience. But she felt her nose and her knees and decided that was not happening. It was just fear, plain and simple.

When the final bell rang, Flora asked Yury to wait outside for her. This being Monday, it was their day to walk together to the bookshop. Yury's eyes got wide when she told him that Mr. Cooper wanted to speak with her, and the look on Yury's face relieved her fear not one bit.

When the room had emptied out, Mr. Cooper asked Flora to come up and sit at a front-row desk. Flora felt so hot that she thought she might faint.

Then Mr. Cooper came around to sit on the edge of his big desk, in front of her, and he gave her a warm and reassuring smile. He had taken some kind of book from his drawer, and now he brought it forth.

"Flora," said Mr. Cooper, "thank you for staying after school an extra few minutes. I wanted to talk to you about this."

He handed Flora the book. It was not a book, though, but a sturdy, thick little magazine. The cover read *CRICKET* in large letters. Beneath that, in smaller letters: *the magazine for children.*

Flora could not guess why she was holding this in her hands, but she was fairly certain now that she was not in trouble, and her temperature started to return to normal.

Flora looked at the magazine, then looked up at Mr. Cooper.

"It is a new publication just for young people," said Mr. Cooper. "Especially young people who love reading and writing."

Flora nodded her head and waited.

"I'm going to loan it to you for a week," said Mr. Cooper. "Then I'll need it back to use in the classroom."

"It's a homework assignment?" asked Flora.

"Oh, no," said Mr. Cooper. "This magazine is an invitation. An invitation for you to be a young writer."

Flora still did not understand. How could a ten-year-old be a writer?

"Look," said Mr. Cooper. He took the magazine from her hands and turned several pages until he found a certain section.

"Here," he said. "These pages are what I want you to think about. Every month the magazine includes stories and poems written by children. See? *Ages nine to twelve.*"

Flora leaned forward as he held up the magazine. She read *Story Contest* and *Poetry Contest*. She looked again at Mr. Cooper.

"Do you mean that I should enter a contest?" she asked. Flora was not very competitive. She was unsure about contests.

"I do," said Mr. Cooper. "Because, Flora, you are a very good writer. And don't worry about the word 'contest.' The magazine chooses winners for every issue. It is not a one-time-only contest. You could send in something every month."

He paused.

"It could be your job," he said with a small laugh.

Flora smiled for the first time in the past hour and ten minutes.

"So take this home," said Mr. Cooper, "and sleep on it, okay?"

"Okay," said Flora. "Thank you, Mr. Cooper."

She wanted to tell him that she enjoyed not only writing but also following the rules. But she decided just to say good-bye and to go find Yury.

He was sitting on the school's front steps.

"What did you *do*?" he asked the moment he saw her.

Flora was slightly offended that Yury obviously thought she had broken a rule. But she could hardly blame him, as she herself had thought the very same thing.

She told Yury about Mr. Cooper and the magazine as they walked to the bookshop.

"That's fantastic," said Yury.

"It is?" asked Flora.

"Of course," said Yury. "Mr. Cooper is telling you something important. He is telling you that you are talented."

"I am not talented," said Flora. "I don't even like the word 'talented.'"

"Okay," said Yury. "Now that I think about it, neither do I. What about 'creative'?"

Flora thought of her father and his photography. She had always considered her father to be creative. Creative seemed much friendlier than talented.

"I can live with that," she said.

Flora looked through the magazine as they walked.

"There are a lot of stories in here by real writers," she said.

"We can read one when we get to the shop," said Yury.

Flora thought a moment.

"No," she said. "We need to remain loyal to the vintage books. I can read the magazine at home. But you may borrow it if you'd like to."

"No, thank you," said Yury. "I'm putting together a Spitfire airplane in my spare time."

As they were nearing the bookshop, Flora could see the dear old books in the display window. Maybe she would write a story for *Cricket*, she thought. Maybe she would even write a book one day. If she did, would someone read it aloud with a friend when it was no longer shiny and new?

She hoped so. Because old was best.

26

The most exciting thing about the April Lyrids was not, for Flora, the shooting stars. Although the nine stars she saw falling out of the sky in streaks of light were each a sudden and happy thrill, the most exciting thing about the April Lyrids was sitting at midnight on reclining webbed lawn chairs in the middle of a farmer's field with both her parents, Forster and Emma Jean. And watching her father grab her mother's hand and hold it tight after the first star fell.

Did he make a wish? thought Flora.

Flora did not make any wishes that night. She was so happy being under that dark sky with her mother and her father that she just could not bring herself to want anything else.

It was in early May when the truly large changes began to take place, and when Flora and her family would become connected to the past in a most unique way.

Flora had spent the night at her father's rented house, and the following morning they decided to walk downtown to the Windy Day Diner for breakfast.

As they made their way along Main Street, passing Wings and a Chair, which was not yet open, and then continuing on another block, Flora's father suddenly stopped next to a storefront that had a large, empty display window. It had been a florist shop, but now it was abandoned.

Flora's father looked at her.

"You will not believe what I am about to tell you," he said.

Though he was smiling, Flora could not help asking, "Is it bad?"

Her father laughed. He had been laughing so much lately. Flora had not realized how his laughter had disappeared for so many months until it came back.

"No, dear, indeed no," said her father. "Not bad. It's good. It's very good."

He faced the large window and spread his arms wide.

"This shop is going to be ours," he said.

"Our shop?" asked Flora.

Her father moved his hand across the span of the plate glass.

"This is going to be ours," he told her. "Mine, yours, and Emma Jean's. Our own shop."

Flora was amazed by what her father was saying. She could hardly absorb it.

Her father told her that in the old days, printers made books and all kinds of printed materials on letterpresses.

He pulled a piece of paper from his pocket. On it was a picture of a large machine with a round disc attached to it and a giant wheel on one side.

"This is an 1890 Chandler and Price letterpress," her father said. "And we bought it!"

"It produces the most beautiful papers," he continued. "Stationery and cards and calendars and journals . . ."

He pointed to the round disc.

"The ink goes there," he said. "And the pieces of paper are fed by hand."

"Did you say 'journals'?" asked Flora. She had decided to write a story for *Cricket* but had not told anyone. A journal would be good for ideas.

"Yes," said her father. "We will design everything ourselves. The letters and decorations are made of lead, and the machine presses them against the paper. You'll see. And you know how your mother loves paper."

Flora did know. Her father had not talked with such excitement in a long time.

"And, Flora," he said, "wait until you see what is upstairs."

"Upstairs?" asked Flora.

She looked up. There were three very tall windows on the second floor, with upper transoms made of stained glass.

"Stained glass," whispered Flora.

"Upstairs will be ours too," said her father.

"Ours?" Flora repeated.

She gazed up at the beautiful windows. The colors were glowing. Someone must have left a light on.

"What is the shop's name?" she asked.

"Rosetown Paper and Press," her father answered.

Flora nodded.

"It's a good name," she said. "Rosetown" was in the name. That is what she would have chosen, too.

Her father gave her a hug.

"We have a lot to do," he said. "But first we need a key!"

27

One of Flora's favorite books in Wings and a Chair was *Meg and the Disappearing Diamonds*. Meg was a girl who solved mysteries, and Flora had read several of the Meg books that Miss Meriwether had been lucky to find. Meg had a cat named Thunder, and this also made Flora feel warmly toward her.

When Flora had read *Meg and the Disappearing Diamonds* in September, so many months ago, two lines from the book had stayed with her. And while lines from books often stayed with Flora, and she often recited them to others, these particular two lines from the Meg story Flora had not shared with anyone. Back then she had been sad about her father's recent move five streets over, sad about having a room in her mother's house and having another room in her father's house when she had once had a room in a house that was *everyone's*. She had wanted someone to cobble the two houses into one so that her family could be together. And when she had read those two lines in the book about Meg, they had sunk deep inside her, where longing was:

Dad had found and restored an old two-story house. Meg loved every wall, floor, and window.

Every wall, floor, and window.

Flora had not imagined, back in September, that something very similar might happen in her own life.

But it had.

During the month of May—after the moving of all the things from the white house back into the yellow house had been accomplished—Flora's parents worked many hours every day and night remodeling the empty shop into a home for Rosetown Paper and Press. Flora's mother loved creamy whites, so every table and chair and cabinet—many pulled from storage in old barns after Flora's father had asked around—was painted a creamy white, which gave the space a warm and open feel.

The front of the shop was for displaying the various correspondence papers, journals, recipe cards, baby announcements, wedding invitations, calling cards, and calendars produced by the printers in the shop (Forster and Emma Jean Smallwood, of course).

And at the back of the shop was the letterpress machine as well as a deep, wide cabinet filled with the lead alphabet letters in many styles and sizes. Each drawer in the cabinet was carefully labeled with its contents: ENGRAVERS TEXT 12 PT and COOPER BLACK 14 PT and dozens of others. Other drawers had all of the lead decorations such as trailing vines and birds and roses.

There were also wide, deep chests of narrow

drawers filled with all of the papers that Emma Jean had carefully chosen, and there were sturdy shelves to hold the many canisters of colored inks.

And upstairs—upstairs was one of Flora's two favorite places in the world (the other being Wings and a Chair Used Books, of course). It was in this large room upstairs with its high tin ceiling, its old oak floors, and its three stained-glass windows that Flora felt she had almost become Meg. For Flora loved every wall, floor, and window.

As did her cat, Serenity. Flora's parents said that this upstairs room would be for "creating and a cat." To this end, the room had only a few pieces of furniture: a long, creamy white table for design work, a few old kitchen chairs pulled up to it, a reading chair with a lamp, and a wicker daybed.

The daybed was for the cat. It was positioned right in front of the tall windows, and from this perch Serenity could look out over the town. She could see people tending their flower gardens. She could see the shopkeepers below, placing their goods on the sidewalk or simply getting some fresh air.

Best of all, she could see the roofs of some of the other downtown buildings where the pigeons would spend their time, plump and gray, keeping a shop cat interested for hours.

Flora's parents planned to keep the shop open for limited hours only: nine o'clock to two o'clock weekdays. They both wanted to keep their regular jobs and to grow the paper shop gradually. "It is barely a sprout," her father said.

Flora was very happy about the limited hours and her mother keeping her part-time job at Wings and a Chair. Flora so loved being there three afternoons a week, and as a girl rooted in tradition, she did not want her time there or her walks after school with Yury to change.

By the end of May, then, it seemed that everyone had projects. Important projects! And not only Flora's parents, who would open Rosetown Paper and Press in July.

Flora also had a project: a story she intended to

write and send to *Cricket* by the end of the summer.

And Nessy had a project: she was finally going to learn to ride a bike. Nessy had resisted bicycles. But Flora told Nessy that if she had a bike, she could put a basket on it, and a bell, and even streamers. So Nessy changed her mind.

And Yury—Yury had so many projects planned for the summer. First and most important, the Beginner's Class at Good Manners for Good Dogs dog school. He could hardly wait. He and Friday would have to do much practicing, so Yury was reserving mornings for his dog. Second, continuing to serve Mo's 24 tea at his father's office in the afternoons. And third, becoming a better bowler than his mother.

Flora and Yury soon would be graduating fourth grade. What a time it had been. Flora felt so lucky that when school had started last fall, and fourth grade had felt so new and daunting, Mr. Cooper had seated the new boy in class at the desk behind hers, a new boy who was Ukrainian, bright, and good.

Serenity had found a home with Flora this past year, and Friday had achieved the status of Beginner Dog.

Flora's father and mother had come apart and then come back together.

And Nessy had been given a canary. She had also discovered that she was very good on piano.

At dusk on the evening before the last day of school, Flora's father took her for a long drive through the countryside, where they could see more of the horizon, more birds, more farms, more sky. They played their favorite Beatles song, "Here Comes the Sun," on her father's cassette player, and every time the song ended, Flora pressed the rewind button and they played it again.

It seemed ages ago that their old dog, Laurence, had passed on, but on the other hand, it seemed to Flora that he really hadn't, and was there with them, in the backseat of the car, his big warm nose smearing up the windows. She would never forget Laurence. He would always go everywhere with her.

Flora and her father listened to the Beatles, ate

Red Hots, counted crows, and, as her father liked to say, watched the corn grow.

Then they turned their car around and went back home.

Home, to Rosetown, Indiana.

A READING GROUP GUIDE TO

Rosetown

by
Cynthia Rylant

Discussion Questions

1. Flora's parents are separated, and now she has two homes with two bedrooms. Despite the fact that she's gained more space to call her own, she still feels a great loss. Why do you think that is? Do you think it's possible to gain something and lose something at the same time? What might you tell Flora to help her feel better about her situation?

2. Flora wonders if there's really a cat hiding under the steps of the barbershop. Yury agrees that the cat exists, saying, "Unless I am delusional. . . . My father says that sometimes I am a master of grand delusion." Flora decides that she's "glad to have a friend capable of grand delusions." What does Flora mean by this? How might Yury share his delusions with her?

3. Standing in the field after meeting Zowie, a parachuting dog, Flora has a feeling that she identifies as "expectation." How would you describe that feeling? What might happen when something doesn't meet your expectations? What might happen when it does? How might either experience change your perception of future expectations? Flora's father did not feel what she felt; he had his "work eyes." Do you think your parent's or caregiver's expectations are different from your own?

4. Although Yury was missing his cat who had passed away, he wanted Flora to have the new cat they'd found. Flora thinks, "it is a rare thing when a friend wants, really wants, you to be happy." Name other scenes in the book that show evidence of Yury, Flora, and Nessy's close friendship. What does it mean to be a good friend?

5. Why does Yury choose "Friday" for his puppy's name? What kind of qualities and personality do you think Yury hopes his puppy will have? Did Friday live up to his name?

6. What does Flora mean when she says she and her mother both loved "good words"? What might they love about the word "thrifty"? Think about whether this is a word you hear often. What are some of your favorite words? How do you learn new words? What do you do when you come across a word and you don't know what it means?

7. When Flora's mother signs her up for piano lessons, Flora realizes that "she had always wanted to play the piano. She just had not known this about herself until now." Have you ever felt this way? How do you learn about your likes and dislikes? Nessy discovers she is also musically talented. What does this discovery mean for Nessy? Why does it make her feel like she belongs to something?

8. What does it mean to be a survivalist? How do Yury and Flora learn more about becoming one? How does Yury use those skills to come to the rescue when Flora and her mother need to get to Wings and a Chair Used Books?

9. Mr. Cooper's "Encyclopedia Hour" fills Flora with a wealth of information about the world. Why is this so exciting to Flora? Why does she plan to use the encyclopedia to learn about whales and dolphins?

10. Yury and his family are from Ukraine. Why did they leave? Is it possible for them to go back? What does Flora learn about his native language, customs, and Christmas celebrations?

11. Miss Meriwether travels to Paris and sends Flora a postcard that says *"Bonjour, mes amis!"* which means "Hello, friends!" in French. If you could travel anywhere in the world, where would you go? What language do they speak there? Flora and her mother visit Miss Meriwether's house and learn that she also used to live in Nepal. What does she teach them about Nepal?

Extension Activities

1. Yury and Flora like to make up stories together by alternating words or phrases. "'I would like to go there,' Yury said, pointing to a book about Key West. 'I would sail a sailboat.' 'And follow an octopus,' said Flora. 'To South America,' said Yury. 'To a town filled with . . . ,' Flora said, then waited for his answer. 'Elephants,' finished Yury." Start a story with your group, having people take turns adding words or phrases as you write them on the board or piece of paper. Once everyone has participated, read the full story aloud. Then make a different writing prompt and have everyone work individually to write a short story based on that prompt. Have people read their short stories out loud to the group. Discuss the differences between collaboration and individual work, and how group members found both experiences. Was it harder working in a group to create a story, or working on their own? Did the first activity help spur creativity for the second? Which activity did they prefer? Relate their experiences to the variety of projects the characters of *Rosetown* plan to embark on at the end of the book. Group endeavors include Flora's parents working together on a new business and Yury helping at his father's office and joining Good Manners for Good Dogs dog school; largely solo endeavors include Flora writing a story and Nessy learning to ride a bike. What are some of the challenges the characters might face? What are some of the benefits of working alone or working together?

2. Flora's name means "flower," and Vanessa's means "butterfly." Have the group look up the origin and meanings of their names, and share them. Discuss the history behind them, and whether they think the name reflects their personalities.

3. Flora and Yury read many vintage books at Wings and a Chair Used Books. Break the large group into small groups and assign each one to a vintage book mentioned in *Rosetown*. Print out the book covers and book summaries for them. Then have them go to the library and find a book in a similar genre for the same age group. Have them compare and contrast the modern and vintage books, looking at the covers, the content, the characters, the setting, and the writing style. Why do they think Flora and Yury loved reading vintage books? How have children's books changed? What might a young reader from the 1970s be surprised to read about in our books?

4. *Rosetown* is set in 1972, just after the Vietnam War. Reread the first chapter where Flora's father talks to her about being "born into an angry world." Why might he have said that? Is the time period important to the story? Is it important to Flora's role in her family? Have group members research events that happened in the month or year they were born, and make a time line together. Discuss the importance of these events, and how they may have affected their families or the country.

5. Flora, Yury, and Nessy try many different activities—some of which they enjoy, and others they decide aren't the best fit for them. Have group members create charts with three columns: Activities I've Tried, Activities I Love, and Activities I Want to Try. Then have them fill out each column. If needed, help them brainstorm a list of activities before beginning. For an additional challenge, have them set goals for trying new activities.